TALES FROM SCHROON LAKE

The Problem
With Prickles

WRITTEN BY
Barbara Davoll
Pictures by Dennis Hockerman

MOODY

To Jack Wyrtzen, encourager and fellow-laborer in the gospel, whose consistent, godly life and ministry at Word of Life International has written the real *Tales from Schroon Lake* and has brought our little dot on the map to the attention of the world.

> *"This book of the law shall not depart out of thy mouth, but thou shalt meditate therein day and night, that thou mayest observe to do according to all that is written therein; for then thou shalt make thy way prosperous, and then thou shalt have good success."*
> *Joshua 1:8*

Moody Press, a ministry of the Moody Bible Institute, is designed for education, evangelization, and edification. If we may assist you in knowing more about Christ and the Christian life, please write us without obligation: Moody Press, c/o MLM, Chicago, IL 60610.

ISBN: 0-8024-1035-9
13579108642
Printed in the United States of America

"Tales From Schroon Lake," is the newest animal adventure series for children written by Barbara Davoll. It takes its setting from the tiny town of Schroon Lake, high in the Adirondack Mountains of upstate New York, where Barbara and her husband, Roy, make their home and serve the Lord with Word of Life International as Children's Representatives. The Davolls are lovingly known around the world as "Uncle Roy and Aunt Barb" as they minister in children's crusades at home and abroad.

Barbara is well known for her award-winning, best-selling Christopher Churchmouse Classics and the Molehole Mystery series. She has allowed her many talents and abilities to be used for the Lord in the areas of writing, composing, teaching, and music, but she loves being a wife, mother, and grandmother and still enjoys being a homemaker for Roy and their schnauzer, Josh.

Illustrator Dennis Hockerman collaborated with friend Barbara Davoll to bring to life a family of lovable churchmice, a captivating underground village of moles, and now a charming band of beavers. Balancing fun-filled imagery with the natural realism of life in a beaver lodge proved to be a real challenge in creating the "Tales From Schroon Lake" series. The artist enjoys viewing the world through a child's eyes and works almost exclusively in the children's market. He lives with his wife, three children, and two Yorkshire terriers in Mequon, Wisconsin, a Milwaukee suburb.

It was a fine summer day. Bucky Beaver
sat on an old tree stump waiting for Razzy Raccoon.
He was looking forward to a long afternoon playing with his
friend. Suddenly something sharp poked
him in the back. "Don't move!
I've got you!" said a
rough voice.

Bucky jumped. The sharp thing poked him again. Then he heard a little giggle. Jerking around he saw Razzy and Prickles Porcupine.

Jumping up quickly, Bucky yelled, "What do you two think you're doing? You nearly scared the life out of me!" He rubbed his shoulder where Razzy had been sticking him with a pine cone.

"Sorry, Bucky. We just couldn't resist when we saw you sitting there," said the porcupine. "Look, we found this pine cone. It's the shape of a football. Let's play."

Just then Reba and Ruby, Razzy's little twin sisters came running out of the woods. "Can we play too?" they yelled, jumping around with excitement.

Bucky looked doubtful. "I don't know," he said slowly. "You might get hurt. Football is a very rough game."

"We can play 'touch' so it won't be too rough for the girls," Razzy suggested. "Let's do it!"

Bucky still looked doubtful. "I don't know, Razzy. Even playing 'touch' with Prickles can be dangerous."

"I'll be careful," promised the porcupine. "Please let me play."

The porcupine was a nice animal, and Bucky liked him. But it was always a challenge to play with him. The porcupine's body was covered with long quills that were as sharp as little razors. Sometimes they let go and stuck in anyone they touched. For that reason many animals feared him. He didn't have many friends.

"Come on, Bucky. Prickles and I will play against you and the girls. We'll even let you have an extra person on your team. How's that?" Razzy was a fun lover and always wanted everyone to have a good time. He was one of the few animals that were friendly to Prickles.

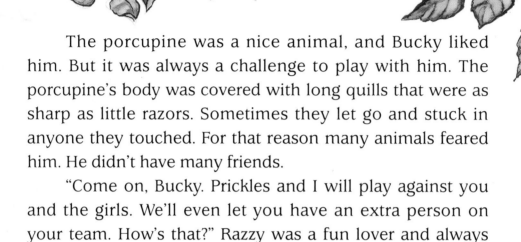

Bucky wanted to play too, but he wished they didn't have to worry about the porcupine's quills. Finally he agreed, and the fun began.

All was going well as they scrambled back and forth carrying the pine cone. Prickles was carrying it and dashing wildly toward his goal when there was an upset.

Razzy's quick little sister Reba ran in front of him from the side, and Prickles fell over her. Razzy and Bucky were right behind. There was no way to stop in time. Razzy fell on top of Prickles, and Bucky fell on top of Razzy.

"Get off, Bucky! Get off!" screamed Razzy. The weight of Bucky's body pressed Razzy down on Prickles and the porcupine's quills bit into the raccoon.

Bucky jumped up from where he had landed on top of the raccoon. He was also in pain. But he had only two or three quills stuck in him. Poor Razzy was covered with them. They were all over him, and several were stuck in his nose.

Reba and Ruby stared in horror at their brother. Bucky jumped around, crying and trying to pull out the quills that were in him.

"I'm sorry, guys," said Prickles with tears in his eyes. "It was an accident. I didn't mean to do it. Let me help you get them out," he offered, reaching toward the quill stuck in Bucky's paw.

Bucky jumped back in alarm. "Don't touch me, Prickles!" he yelled. "You'll get another one in me!"

Ruby ran to call her parents.

The raccoon home wasn't far away, and in just a few minutes Father and Mother Raccoon were on the scene. Mother attended to Razzy. Father helped Bucky pull out the quills stuck in him.

Mother Raccoon helped Razzy to a stump, where he sat down. She began to pull out the quills. Each one cut like a knife.

Bucky stood nearby sniffing and rubbing his leg where the quills had hurt him.

"Reba, run over to Doctor Owl and ask him to come quickly. I'll need some medicine right away," said Mother Raccoon. Reba took off running, glad for the opportunity to do something to help.

Prickles stood by crying as he realized how seriously Razzy was hurt.

"We know you didn't mean to hurt him, Prickles," Father Raccoon said soothingly. He was trying to hold Razzy still as Mother pulled the quills out.

"I'm not going to play with Prickles anymore," said little Ruby with tears rolling down her face. "It's too d-d-dangerous," she cried, stumbling over the big word she had heard Bucky use. She loved her big brother and couldn't stand to see him hurt.

Prickles began to cry harder. Turning around blindly, he ran right into Bucky.

"For pete's sake, Prickles! Watch where you're going! You almost got me again!" yelled Bucky, jumping back quickly to avoid the porky's quills.

At that Prickles started for home. He knew he wasn't wanted.

"What's keeping Dr. Owl?" worried Father Raccoon, looking up at the sky. "I thought he would be here by now."

"Maybe he's with another patient." Mother Raccoon pulled another quill free.

Suddenly Bucky realized that Prickles was gone. He knew the porcupine felt terrible about what had happened. *I've got to find him and tell him it's all right,* thought Bucky.

Just then a dark shadow appeared overhead. Looking up, Bucky saw Dr. Owl flying in with his black bag in his beak. The owl swooped low and landed.

Now's my chance to go look for Prickles, thought Bucky. He knew Razzy was in good hands with his parents and the owl doctor.

Hurrying down the wooded path leading to Beaver Falls, Bucky thought he would likely find Prickles up in his favorite tree. As he ran along he met Reba, coming back from getting Dr. Owl.

"Dr. Owl is already with Razzy," he explained. "Too bad you can't fly, or you'd be there too," he joked.

Reba didn't laugh. She was too worried about Razzy.

"He'll be all right, Reba. Your mother is pulling the quills out, and Dr. Owl will put medicine on him. He'll be fine."

The little girl raccoon wiped her eyes and snuffled. "Yes, but he wouldn't have been hurt if we hadn't played with Prickles." She sniffed. Tears rolled down her furry face from her little black masked eyes.

"I know, but accidents do happen," responded the beaver gently. He patted her shoulder awkwardly.

"That old Prickles! He shouldn't be around other animals," stormed Razzy's angry little sister, stamping her foot. "Porcupines are *no good*!"

"He's really a very nice animal, Reba. It was more our fault than his. It just wasn't wise to play football. He didn't mean to hurt Razzy."

Bucky could see his words had little effect on Reba. She stood with her head bent, still crying.

"He's really very sorry, Reba," continued Bucky. "He went home crying. I was just going to look for him so he won't feel so bad."

"Well, I hope he *does feel bad. Real bad!*" she yelled and stomped off.

Bucky sighed and continued on his way. When he found Prickles he could not convince the porcupine that all would be well. Prickles was brokenhearted.

"I *hate being a porcupine!*" he told Bucky. "It just isn't fair!"

It was a very difficult time for Bucky. When Chatty Chipmunk heard what happened, she made up bad stories about Prickles. Bucky tried to convince the forest folk that Prickles was really a good and gentle animal. But none of them believed him. No one would give Prickles a chance.

And to make matters worse, Razzy became unfriendly to Bucky. Somehow the raccoon blamed Bucky for his problem with Prickles.

One moonlit night Bucky and his family were cutting trees near the shore of Schroon Lake. Razzy and his family were fishing on the beach. Bucky wished things were like they used to be when he and Razzy were better friends. Then Bucky might have been fishing *with* them.

Taking a break from the hard job of lumberjack, Bucky straightened up and mopped his forehead with his neckcloth. As he did, he looked through the trees and watched Razzy's family.

It was fun to watch the raccoons catch fish and then carefully wash each bite before they ate. They were such interesting animals.

As Bucky watched, he suddenly drew in his breath and began to shake. Something was creeping out of the woods behind the raccoon family. It was a huge black bear!

"Father! L-look! It's a b-bear," he stammered in a hoarse whisper. Bucky was so frightened he could hardly get the words out.

Father dropped the branch he was carrying and stared down the beach. "Don't move!" he commanded.

"But, Father! He'll get Razzy's family! What can we do?" cried Bucky wildly. "We must warn them." He started to run toward the raccoons.

"Stop, Bucky! We're no match for a bear. All we can do is thump our tails."

Father and then Bucky began to thump their tails on the ground. This was a danger signal the entire animal world understood.

The moment the raccoons heard the beavers thumping, they stopped fishing and looked up. But it was too late! The bear was almost upon them. They backed into the water trying to get away, but he was right after them.

Plunging into the lake, the bear first swiped his big paw at little Reba, who screamed with terror and jumped away.

With a tremendous roar that shook the trees, the bear next grabbed for Razzy. He brushed him with his big paw, and Razzy flew out of the water onto the beach. The bear lunged after him.

It was all happening right before Bucky's eyes. The little beaver hid his face in his paws. He couldn't stand to watch.

Suddenly it happened! Out of the woods appeared a small, round form that looked more like a prickly ball than an animal. With a growl the ball moved straight toward the big black bear, who now turned away from Razzy. There was a scream from the bear as Prickles Porcupine turned around and let loose his armor of quills.

Roaring and screaming in pain, the bear plunged blindly into the forest. His soft nose and face were full of porcupine quills. He wouldn't bother the raccoons now.

"Bucky! Prickles has saved the raccoon family," Father Beaver said, putting his paw on his little beaver's shoulder.

Bucky was still shaking. Taking his paws from his face, Bucky could hardly believe what he saw. Father and Mother

Raccoon were safely walking up the beach toward the beavers. They were carrying the twins. Razzy was limping ahead of them and seemed to be all right.

"Bucky! Bucky! Did you see what happened?" yelled Razzy breathlessly. "Prickles saved our lives. That bear almost had us!"

Bucky ran to meet his friend. "I know! I know, Razzy! Are you all right?" He grabbed his friend and gave him a hug. "We tried to warn you by thumping our tails, but it was too late. I thought you were goners for sure!"

"He-he got my leg a little, but not bad. Can you believe that porcupine, Bucky? Wasn't he something? He just stormed right out there and let those old quills go! I guess there's some good in a porcupine after all." Razzy just couldn't stop talking about their lifesaver, Prickles. By this time the raccoon family had reached Father and Mother Beaver.

"Look, Father! Isn't that Prickles over there in the trees?" Ruby excitedly pointed toward the woods. Sure enough, a little prickly ball was peering out at them.

"I'll go get him," said Reba, jumping out of Mother Raccoon's arms. "Prickles! Come on out! Our family wants to thank you for saving our lives! We're all sorry for how we treated you."

It took a little convincing for the shy, gentle porky to come with her. But when he did, there was much rejoicing.

Mother Raccoon wiped her eyes on her apron as she stood with Mother Beaver. Both mothers were thinking what could have happened if Prickles had not done his work so bravely.

"Oh, Prickles, I'd just love to give you a big hug," said Mother Raccoon. "But—how can I do that?" She looked at his quills.

"Aw, it's easy. You just hug from a distance like this," he said, leaning over and placing his paws gently on Mother Raccoon's paws. She laughed and carefully leaned closer to him.

"That'll work," Razzy laughed. "We just have to learn how to manage him and his prickles."

"I don't think that will be too hard," said Father Raccoon. "We've certainly learned tonight that his quills are very important. He has them for a good reason.

"I guess so," Bucky said with a smile. "Now that we understand how his quills work, maybe we all can play together."

"Right!" said Razzy, looking at his friend Bucky. "Now we can *all* play together again."

"But not football," joked Prickles.

"Not even 'touch,'" said Reba.

"No, I don't think football's a good idea," agreed Mother Raccoon. "But how about some crayfish crumpets and tea at our house?"

The beavers, raccoons, and porcupine all thought that was a great suggestion.

BUCKY'S

BELIEVE IT OR NOT

The porcupine has 33,000 quills that are sharp as a razor.

Porcupines spend a lot of
time sleeping and sunning
themselves in the tops of tall trees.

Porcupines are born in a little sack so that their quills won't hurt their mothers.

A beaver cuts down between two and three hundred trees a year.

BEAVER TAILS

Have you ever seen a porcupine? They look just like balls of prickly needles with eyes. They can't run very fast, but they don't need to. They have only one thing to use to defend themselves against their enemies. That is their quills.

God has given *us* something to defend ourselves against the bad guy Satan. The Lord has given us the Word of God. It is an armor to protect us from Satan's attacks.

Ephesians 6:11 says, "Put on the whole armor (or covering) of God that you may be able to stand firm against the schemes (or attacks) of the devil." You can put on God's armor by reading the Bible and memorizing it.

Do you have a friend like Prickles who has some "prickly" ways and is hard to be around? By reading the Word of God you can learn how to be a loyal, encouraging friend like Bucky and get along with prickly people. Just as God gave Prickles his quills, God has given us His Word to help us live.